Her own wings

The Little Angel of Honesty smiled to herself. Celine. That was the name of the girl she was supposed to help. What a lovely name. This Celine apparently had a terrible problem.

The archangel had told the little angel that she would almost certainly earn enough feathers from this task to have her own wings. The little angel wanted to laugh—her own wings. Then it wouldn't matter how small or tall anyone was— when you flew, you could see everything everywhere. Oh, how she longed to fly.

Aladdin

Angelwings

No. 9

Lies and
Lemons

Donna Jo Napoli

illustrations by Lauren Klementz-Harte

Aladdin Paperbacks
New York London Toronto Sydney Singapore

Thank you to all my family,
Brenda Bowen, Cylin Busby, Nöelle Paffett-Lugassy,
Karen Riskin, and Richard Tchen

First Aladdin Paperbacks edition May 2000

Text copyright © 2000 by Donna Jo Napoli
Illustrations copyright © 2000 by Lauren Klementz-Harte

Aladdin Paperbacks
An imprint of Simon & Schuster
Children's Publishing Division
1230 Avenue of the Americas
New York, NY 10020

Designed by Steve Scott
The text for this book was set in Cheltenham and Minister Light.
The illustrations were rendered in ink and wash.
Printed and bound in the United States of America
2 4 6 8 10 9 7 5 3 1

Library of Congress Cataloging-in-Publication Data
Napoli, Donna Jo, 1948–
Lies and lemons / Donna Jo Napoli ;
illustrations by Lauren Klementz-Harte
— 1st Aladdin Paperbacks ed.
p.   cm. — (Aladdin Angelwings ; 9)
Summary: The Little Angel of Honesty hopes to understand why Celine continually twists the truth so that she can help her and earn her wings.
ISBN 0-689-83209-5 (pbk.)
[1. Angels—Fiction. 2. Honesty—Fiction.]
I. Klementz-Harte, Lauren, 1961–   II. Title.
PZ7.N15 Lf 2000
[Fic]—dc21   99-87417

For Nick,
the Champion of Truth

Aladdin
Angelwings
№. 9

Lies and
Lemons

Angel Talk

Out of the corner of her eye, the Little Angel of Honesty saw the Archangel of Honesty waving both hands. She bowed her head and kept talking to her friends, pretending she hadn't noticed.

The archangel quickly walked up to the group of little angels. "Hurry," she whispered in the ear of the littlest angel.

"Oh, you can talk out loud," said the Little Angel of Honesty. She got to her feet and stood on tiptoe. That way maybe the others wouldn't notice how short she was. "They all know that I have a big task to do."

The archangel gave a small smile. "And do they know that you're late? You were supposed to meet me at dawn."

The littlest angel looked around at her

1

friends. "I have to go now. To Venice. Bye." She put a bag of lemon drops on the lap of the nearest little angel.

"Ooo, lemon drops. Yum," said the little angel.

"Try them, all of you. They taste great," said the Little Angel of Honesty. "But they smell even better."

"Thanks. Don't drown in a canal," said one of the other little angels.

"And bring us back something made of that wonderful Italian blown glass. Maybe a family of little animals," said a third little angel.

"Or a glass angel," said a fourth little angel.

"Perfect," they all murmured together.

The archangel looked at them in confusion. "But we're not—"

"We have to rush," said the Little Angel of Honesty. She grabbed the archangel's hand and pulled her along, running and waving behind at her friends.

"Now you're all for speed," said the

archangel, practically stumbling. "We don't have to go that fast. Please slow down."

The Little Angel of Honesty slowed to a fast walk, but she still kept pulling the archangel.

"Little angel, you do realize we're not going to Venice, Italy. We're only going to Venice, California. It's right near that wonderful city named just for us: Los Angeles. I thought I explained that to you."

"You did." The little angel flicked a speck of lint off her gown and marched ahead.

"But your friends think you're going off to Italy," said the archangel.

"Yup."

The Archangel of Honesty stopped, still holding the little angel's hand, so that the little angel jerked to a halt. "You lied to them, little angel."

"No I didn't. I just didn't explain it. They don't have to know that it's Venice, California."

"But that's the equivalent of a lie."

"No it isn't. They think what they want to think. It's more fun for them that way. Here, have a lemon drop." The little angel put a candy in the archangel's hand and held another one up to her nose. "Don't they smell like bright tropical days on the Mediterranean Sea?"

"Little angel . . . "

"Hurry." The little angel put the rest of her candy back in her pocket, grabbed the archangel's hand again, and ran. "Aren't we supposed to get there early?"

"We really do need to talk about this," said the archangel between puffs of breath. "But, you're right, we really do need to hurry, too. Celine will be off to school soon." She put the lemon drop in her mouth. "Thanks for the candy."

The Little Angel of Honesty smiled to herself. Celine. That was the name of the girl she was supposed to help. What a lovely name. This Celine apparently had a terrible problem.

The archangel had told the little angel that she would almost certainly earn enough feathers from this task to have her own wings. The little angel wanted to laugh—her own wings. Then it wouldn't matter how small or tall anyone was—when you flew, you could see everything everywhere. Oh, how she longed to fly.

A bell would ring when the Little Angel of Honesty earned those wings, just as a bell rang whenever any little angel finally got her wings. The Little Angel of Honesty imagined herself flying over the famous square in Venice, Italy, the one that's in so many pictures, with the pink palace and the gilded church and the tall bell tower. Oh, if only the bell in that tower could ring for the little angel.

Oatmeal

Celine looked at the bowl of oatmeal. "It's gray and lumpy."

"Disgusting," agreed Michael. "Eat it." He took another huge bite of his bagel.

"This isn't fair," said Celine. "You get to choose what you want, and I have to eat whatever Ma makes me."

"That's 'cause you're little and I'm big. She doesn't boss me around anymore."

Celine wrinkled her nose. "It's already getting cold and slimy on top."

"Here." Michael dug a raisin out of his bagel and threw it on top of Celine's oatmeal.

"Yuck. It looks like a dead bug."

"Raisins are good," said Michael. Then he smiled. "And they're good for you," he said in a tone that mimicked Ma. He picked up his backpack. "Hurry up or you'll miss the bus."

"I'm walking."

"Suit yourself," called Michael. Celine heard the door open and shut.

That raisin really did look like a bug. Celine picked it out of her oatmeal and ate it. Then she ran into Michael's bedroom.

Racine sat unmoving in the corner of his huge glass tank, his big legs spread out in a circle. Michael said Racine was a perfect name for this spider, but Celine knew Michael had chosen to name the spider Racine because that name ended like her own: Racine, Celine—they sounded sort of alike. She hated spiders, and Michael knew that. Maybe Celine should change her own name to Susie.

Racine looked like a tarantula. Everyone that saw him for the first time said, "Oh, a tarantula." Then Michael would explain that real tarantulas are poisonous and they

come from Italy. Most giant, hairy spiders aren't dangerous like tarantulas. Racine was a Chilean red-leg. He was now only a little over two and a half inches with his legs extended. But he could grow to as much as ten inches. Racine was just a baby. Or sort of a baby. He ate flies and crickets and whatever icky things Michael caught for him—especially roaches, which Michael caught in a stupid box called a Roach Motel. When Racine got bigger, he'd eat mice and small birds. Ma said that when he got that big, Michael would have to get rid of him. That wasn't because she liked mice. Ma hated mice. It was because Racine was a messy eater, and Ma didn't want to think about what his tank would look like if he ate mice and birds.

But right now Celine was grateful Racine was a messy eater. That was part of her plan. She looked through the mess of leaves on the bottom of the tank. Yup, there were lots of roach parts here and there. She went over to Michael's desk and got an index card. Then she used it to scoop up the roach pieces.

Racine just watched in his crazy multiple-eyed way. He seemed almost nice, as though he was saying, "Go ahead, help yourself."

Celine went into the kitchen and tilted the index card so the roach pieces slid onto the top of her oatmeal. "Ma!" she screamed.

Ma came rushing into the kitchen.

"Look!"

"What is that?"

"It looks like insect body parts to me," said Celine.

"How disgusting." Ma dumped the bowl of oatmeal down the garbage disposal. "I'll make you a fresh bowl."

"I'll miss the bus. Can't I just take a bagel and run?"

"Well, all right. This once." Ma dropped half a bagel into the toaster.

Celine put on her backpack and got out

the cream cheese. As the bagel popped up, she plucked it out and smeared it with cream cheese. "Bye, Ma. Thanks." She ran for the door.

Angel Talk

The Archangel of Honesty gave a little sniff of disapproval.

"I agree. That was awful." The Little Angel of Honesty shuddered. "What if that spider had jumped up and bit her?"

"That's not a real Italian tarantula," said the archangel. "I've heard Michael talk about it. It's harmless to people."

"Really? Wow, I'm going to collect some of the hairs lying in his tank so I can show all the other little angels later."

The archangel tapped her finger on her lips. "So you can fool them into thinking you really did go to Italy?"

"I didn't say that. Anyway, they'd get a thrill out of seeing the hairs if they thought they were real tarantula hairs. They'd be all excited."

'And you'd be the center of attention," said the archangel.

The Little Angel of Honesty frowned. "We're supposed to be talking about Celine, not me."

"You're right. Celine has a serious problem: She fooled her mother."

"Well, wouldn't you? Her brother got a delicious bagel, and all she got was that slop."

"Oatmeal isn't slop." The archangel sniffed again. "I happen to like oatmeal. Very much."

"Celine doesn't. Her mother's mean."

"How can you say that? You don't know anything about her mother."

"I can tell. Her brother seems nice enough, though." The little angel stood on her toes. "Celine is sort of tall, isn't she? I'd love to be tall like that."

"You're fine just the size you are," said the archangel. "And if you want us to talk about Celine and not you, then keep your mind on the problem, please."

"I don't really see a problem. All she did was trick her mother a bit so that she could have a good breakfast. It didn't hurt anyone."

"Are you sure about that?"

The little angel blinked. "Well, Celine did cause her mother to waste a bowl of food. But that's not really a big deal."

The Archangel of Honesty looked thoughtful. "And what about what Celine did to herself?" she asked gently.

"What do you mean?"

"I suspect there's more to this than just the choice of oatmeal or a bagel." The archangel tapped her lips again. "Yes, little angel, I suspect there's a whole lot more going on."

Overalls

Celine ran down the street, but before she got to the bus stop, she turned and ducked into Ellen's garage.

"What took you so long?" Ellen handed Celine a plastic bag. "We're going to miss the bus."

"We can walk." Celine opened the bag and shook out the new overalls. They were denim with huge pockets and a loop for a hammer.

"I don't like to walk," said Ellen.

Celine yanked off her skirt and pulled on the overalls. They were so floppy, they felt funny. She walked with her legs splayed. "How did you get used to yours?"

"Practice." Ellen marched around Celine, looking totally preoccupied, as if she was off to rake the leaves or take out the garbage.

"Well, it's a good thing we're walking to school, then. That'll give me time to practice." Celine stuffed her skirt into the plastic bag and stashed the bag in the corner of the garage. "Let's go."

Ellen was right: Within minutes Celine felt comfortable in the overalls. She varied her stride—longer, then shorter, fast, then slow. What wonderful overalls these were.

"There's your mom," said Ellen.

Celine was so startled, she knocked into Ellen and they both almost fell. Ma drove by and stopped at the stop sign on the corner. She must not have recognized Celine from behind in the overalls. But what if she looked in the rearview mirror now? Celine whipped off her backpack and held it in front of her face.

"Are you crazy?"

"If she sees me in these overalls, she'll make me take them off," said Celine. "She thinks overalls are sloppy, and she'd die if she knew I had any."

"Hi, Celine," said Cara, catching up on the left.

"Don't talk to me," said Celine. "I'm hiding." Then she got all flustered. After all, Cara seemed nice, even though they hardly ever talked. "Hey," she said, "call me Susie from now on."

"Oh." Cara walked on.

Ellen tugged at Celine's backpack. "Your mom's gone. Don't act so stupid."

Celine slung her backpack over one shoulder so it was ready to slap in front of her face again if Ma should happen to make a U-turn and come on back. "Your mother lets you wear anything you want. You don't understand."

"Of course I understand. What I meant was that holding up your backpack was dumb. If you're trying not to be seen, you shouldn't draw attention to yourself."

"Oh. Yeah. You're right." Celine laughed. She took Ellen's hand. "Let's run the rest of the way."

Angel Talk

"See? What did I tell you?" The Archangel of Honesty coughed modestly into her hand.

"Want a lemon drop for your cough?" The little angel held out a bag of the candies.

"Thank you. I feared Celine would do something like this."

"All she did was hide her new overalls in her friend's garage. There's nothing wrong with that. Didn't you like the way Ellen and Celine walked in their overalls?" The little angel strode around the archangel.

"But, little angel, Celine's being naughty. Her mother doesn't want her wearing overalls."

"Her mother has a problem." The Little Angel of Honesty posed with a hand on one

hip, then on the other. "I'd look good in overalls, I bet. They make you seem larger. Anyone is noticeable in overalls."

"Maybe it's time for us to have that little talk about you," said the archangel.

The littlest angel dropped her hands. "No. I want to talk about Celine."

"All right, then." The archangel took the little angel's hands. "Celine has been dishonest to her mother twice today."

"Not exactly," said the little angel, pulling away and striding around the archangel again, but slowly this time. "After all, her mother didn't ask how the roach parts got in the oatmeal, and she doesn't even know enough to ask Celine if she's got overalls. Celine hasn't said anything untrue."

"It's not just what people say. You know that." The archangel turned in a circle so that she could keep her eyes on the little angel, who was still walking around her. "Celine's mother believes Celine just happened to find the insect parts in her food this morning. And she believes Celine is wearing her skirt to school today."

"So what?"

"Stop walking; you're making me dizzy."

The little angel stopped and drew circles with the tips of her right toes. She kept her eyes on the ground.

"Celine has led her mother to believe that things are different from the way they really are." The archangel's voice got very quiet. "That's what. You know how these things can happen," she added almost in a whisper.

The little angel looked up at the archangel and remembered how the other little angels thought she'd gone off to Italy instead of California. "All right. I see what you mean. But, really, what's the harm in it? Celine's mother is happier not knowing."

"Do you really believe that?"

"Celine believes it. Why else would she do it?"

"That's what you need to figure out," said the archangel. "Because once you figure it out, I think you'll have a better chance of helping her stop it."

Susie

Russ did three forward rolls, which brought him all the way from the starting rock to the tree that they used as their finish marker. He got up and went to the end of the line. Thomas stuck out his arms as wide as possible and hopped on one foot the entire distance. Ellen did two cartwheels, and her legs were almost straight.

Celine was next. She did a backward roll. She stood up and did a forward roll. Then she ended with a giant leap and ran to the end of the line.

Acrobatics was more fun on a mat. But the gym teacher refused to let them drag one outside to the playground. So the grass had to do—the stiff, scratchy grass. It was okay, though, because Celine's new overalls were so

thick, they protected her; the grass couldn't poke too hard through them.

"Nice," someone said. That was Michael's voice. He was suddenly standing right beside her.

Celine's face got hot. Her brother didn't say anything about her overalls. Well, okay, she'd act like it was nothing special, either. "What are you doing over here? Your class never comes out on this playground."

"I was on my way to play basketball when I thought I smelled something. Lemon, I think. It was so strong. And I looked this way and saw you doing somersaults."

"In acrobatics they're called 'forward rolls' and 'backward rolls,'" said Celine.

"Why is everyone doing acrobatics?"

"We're being judged on our routines in gym class today. So we're practicing."

"You looked good. Especially in that leap at the end. Especially in those overalls." Michael raised an eyebrow. He had just learned how to do that, and Celine knew he loved the opportunity to practice.

"Don't tell Ma."

"Where'd you get them?"

"I bought them. I saved my allowance." Celine jumped in a circle. "Do you really think they look good?"

"Yeah."

"Hi, Susie," said Cara. She walked up and stood there, expectantly.

"Who's Susie?" asked Michael.

"Your sister," said Cara. Then she looked at Celine. "Why did you change your name to Susie? That's such a plain name. You could have chosen Samantha or Jasmine."

"Lots of people go by their middle name," said Celine.

"Oh. Well, then . . . want to watch me do the crab walk?" Cara squatted and walked off all scrunched up and crazy like a crab.

"Your middle name's not Susie," Michael said quietly to Celine.

Celine shrugged. "You never should have named your vicious tarantula after me. I had to change my name."

"Racine's not a tarantula, and you know it. Besides, I named him after a French playwright from the sixteen hundreds."

"You think you're so smart now that you get to take French in school."

"No I don't. I was always smart." Michael laughed. "And Racine has always been sweet. Not like you, you little liar." He shook his head. "Watch out or you'll become a pathological liar." He walked away with his hands in his pockets.

"I'm not . . . " Celine looked around. Michael was too far to hear unless she shouted. And she wasn't about to shout the word "liar."

But the word shouted, anyway, inside her head.

Angel Talk

W hat's a pathological liar?" asked the little angel.

"Someone who lies all the time automatically."

"Well that's not what Celine does. I don't know anyone who does that. No one." The littlest angel stamped her foot. "I've changed my mind; her brother isn't nice after all. He should mind his own business."

"Michael smelled lemons," said the archangel with a suspicious glance at the little angel. "Aren't you the one who made him go over to Celine in the first place?"

"Oh, yeah." The Little Angel of Honesty flushed. "I forgot. I led him by the nose with a lemon drop. I thought he might talk to her about her overalls and help somehow." She held out a lemon drop to the archangel.

They both popped them in their mouths and thought a while.

"So why did Celine tell Cara that her middle name is Susie?" asked the Archangel of Honesty.

"Let's get this straight," said the little angel. "She didn't tell Cara that at all. She merely said that many people go by their middle names, and she let Cara come to the conclusion that her middle name was Susie."

"Okay. Be technical about it." The archangel tossed her hair over one shoulder and divided it into three bunches. She braided it tightly. "Why did she do that?"

"I don't know. What she did with her mother at least made sense. She wanted a bagel and she wanted to wear overalls, and her mother didn't want either thing. But Cara's different. Cara couldn't stop Celine from calling herself Susie or anything else she wants. So I have no idea why Celine did that."

"Michael can't figure it out, either." The archangel finished her braid and patted the tip of it. "She deceives people."

"Not all the time, though," said the little angel. "And I bet not everyone. This is turning out to be a lot harder than I ever expected. Celine's complicated."

The archangel caressed the little angel's cheek. "Isn't everyone?"

Ants

Celine and Ellen scooted to the end of the bench nearest the window so that they were fully in the sun. They took out their sandwiches and ate in quiet companionship.

"It's so nice to be hungry," said Ellen. "Because then you can eat and feel satisfied and fat."

Celine thought about that. Ellen had a point. Celine had never enjoyed hunger before, but now it would become a pleasure. Ha. All because she could look ahead to eating.

But animals probably didn't feel that way. Animals probably just suffered when they were hungry. Animals like Racine.

Celine had been feeling bad about Racine ever since she'd called him vicious when she

32

was talking to Michael. Now she felt even more guilty. Celine hadn't seen any other insect body parts in his tank. What if Racine had nothing left to eat today? "Do you think spiders can suffer?"

"Sure. Anything alive can suffer." Ellen took a bite of carrot. "I mean, even this carrot must have feelings of some sort. So I'm glad it's dead."

"How do you know it's dead?"

"Well, look, it doesn't have any top part on it anymore. It can't be alive."

"I'm not so sure about that," said Celine. "Maybe if you planted it, it would grow again."

Ellen held what remained of her carrot at arm's length and stared at it. "All right. Let's plant it and see."

Celine put her plum in her right front pocket and her celery sticks in her left front pocket and her bag of peanuts in her right hip pocket. She threw her empty lunch bag in the garbage and followed Ellen out to the playground. Ellen's pockets bulged nicely, too. Overalls were certainly handy.

Lunch recess was short, so they had to hurry. They ran to the very corner of the school property.

Ellen found a sharp stone and dug a hole. She planted the half carrot. Then she sat back on her heels. "Look at all those ants. Do you think the point of ants is to squish them?"

"What? You just said anything alive can suffer. Ants are alive." Celine watched the swarming anthill.

"Sure. But you know what I mean. They make you want to squish them."

"Right now I want to catch them." Celine stood up with sudden determination. "I've got to find a container. I know: a milk carton. Stay here and don't let anything happen to those ants." She ran back to the cafeteria, snatched a milk carton out of the trash, and came racing to the anthill again.

Celine put the carton on its side and pushed ants into it. "Help me."

"Why?" But Ellen was already scooping ants into the carton.

"They'll make a tasty little snack for Racine." An ant ran up Celine's arm and under her sleeve. She reached up and brushed it away. "They're hard to control."

"They're climbing all over me." Ellen stood up and swept her hands down her arms wildly. She jumped from foot to foot, as though her whole body were crawling with ants. "Yuck."

"What's going on?"

Both girls spun around.

Mrs. Marcy, their teacher from last year, stood with one hand shading her eyes, watching them. "Why are you putting ants in that milk carton?"

"It takes a lot of ants to make an ant farm," said Celine.

"Oh. How nice. I love ant farms."

Celine knew that, of course. Mrs. Marcy

had a giant ant farm in her classroom.

"Well, I hope you've got everything already arranged for them at home. An aquarium and dirt and . . . "

"I have everything they'll need," said Celine, thinking of Racine's mouth.

"Well, good." Mrs. Marcy smiled and turned to go, then she hesitated. "Have you two been drinking lemonade?"

"No," yelped Ellen. "No no no."

Celine stared at Ellen.

Mrs. Marcy looked surprised, too. "I just thought I smelled lemons. Hmm. Well, bye now." She left.

When she was out of hearing range, Celine asked, "Why'd you shout no?"

"I didn't want to give you a chance to answer," said Ellen.

"Why not?"

"Because you might tell another lie. You're not making an ant farm. You're making a meal for a spider."

At the word "lie," Celine winced. Two people had accused her of lying today. "I couldn't tell Mrs. Marcy that. She loves ants." Celine pushed an escaping ant back into the milk carton and folded the top shut. "She thinks ants are the best thing in the world."

"No one thinks ants are the best thing in the world." Ellen brushed off her hands. "I hate them now, they're so crawly. You should have told Mrs. Marcy that Racine needed a snack. She'd understand."

"What if she didn't?"

"Well, so what?"

"So what? How can you say that? I'd have to argue, then, and I hate arguing." Celine took out her celery sticks and jammed the milk carton full of ants into that pocket. She turned it on its side so that her pocket kept the top closed tight. "Want a celery stick?"

Angel Talk

"Did you make that teacher go up to the girls?" asked the Archangel of Honesty.

"Yes. It's so funny how easy it is to make people follow their noses."

"Did you know that teacher liked ants?" The archangel's voice trembled a little. "Because if you did, then you really set up poor Celine to tell a lie."

"I'd never do that," said the little angel. "I swear. She was just any old teacher, as far as I was concerned. I led her to the girls so I could see how Celine would act around her. The more different people I see Celine with, the better chance I have of understanding her." The little angel pressed her hand to her forehead, which throbbed now, she was so upset. "I

39

never would have chosen that teacher if I'd known."

"It's all right. Don't fret." The archangel took the little angel's hand in one of hers, then smoothed her forehead with the other. "Did you learn anything from seeing how Celine acted with the teacher?"

"Yes." The little angel looked up into the archangel's face. "She doesn't mean to deceive anyone. She just doesn't like to argue."

"That's what she said." The archangel folded her hands behind her and walked.

The little angel ran to catch up. "But you don't think that's the whole story?"

"Do you?"

"Now that I think about it, she did sort of argue with her brother." The little angel folded her own hands behind her, just like the archangel. She took big steps, so that they stayed side by side. "So there's more to it than just arguing. And I'm going to find out what."

Racine

"Let's get off here." Celine got to her feet.

Ellen looked out the bus window. "But this isn't our stop. We still have one to go."

"We're getting off here." Celine walked to the front of the bus. She looked over her shoulder and mouthed "please" as big as she could.

Ellen got up and followed Celine off the bus. "What's up?"

"This way we can go up the block behind your house and cut through Mr. Anton's yard to your garage."

"Why?"

"In case Ma drives by again." Celine looked around furtively. Then she turned up Grant Street.

Ellen walked beside her silently.

Celine turned onto Mr. Anton's yard and ran her hand along the hedge as she hurried across into the back of Ellen's yard. She came up to the rear of the garage and went in through the back door. Safe at last.

Ellen came in behind her and shut the door.

Celine changed in the shadows of the rear of the garage. Then she folded her overalls, carefully smoothing each leg and rolling up the straps. She put them in the plastic bag in the corner again. "What's the matter, Ellen?"

"Huh?"

"You haven't said a word since we got off the bus."

"Neither have you."

Celine held the milk carton with both hands. "Want to help me feed these ants to Racine?"

Ellen shook her head. "Do you smell it?"

"What?"

"Lemons."

At morning recess Michael had talked

about smelling lemons. Then he'd called Celine a liar. And at lunch recess Mrs. Marcy had asked about lemonade. Then Ellen had called Celine a liar. "I don't like the smell of lemons," Celine said.

"It's a nice smell. Clean," said Ellen. "But I can't figure out where it's coming from. It's like it's right in front of my nose and it's been there since we got off the bus." She walked close and sniffed at Celine.

"It's not my fault." Celine quickly backed up. "I'm not a lemon. I hate lemons." She went out the front of the garage. "I've got to run. See you tomorrow."

Ma's car was gone.

Celine got the key out of the secret compartment under the mailbox and let herself in. She wasn't worried about being home alone, because Michael would be back from track practice on the next bus.

She put her backpack away and went directly into Michael's room.

Racine sat in a little well of leaves facing the door, almost as though he were waiting for her.

Celine put down the milk carton. "Are you hungry?"

Racine didn't move.

"You're so weird, the way you just wait all day." Celine took a pencil off Michael's desk and tapped a leaf beside Racine.

The spider seemed to jump to attention.

Celine used the pencil to tap a front leg.

Racine spun around so his rear faced the pencil. With his hindmost legs he tore hairs off his back and flung them at the pencil.

Celine laughed. Then she stopped. "Oh, you funny little thing. You think the pencil's attacking you, don't you?" She put the pencil back on Michael's desk. "I'm sorry. I didn't mean to frighten you. And I've got a treat for you." She picked up the milk carton, but the top had sprung open and ants crawled out and down the sides and all over the little table that Racine's tank perched on. "Oh, no." Celine swept one hand across the table, brushing the ants into her other hand. Then she brushed them off into Racine's tank. But there were still so many crawling all around.

"What are you doing?"

Celine gasped at Michael. "You're not supposed to be home yet."

"Just what are you doing? There are ants everywhere."

"I'm giving Racine a snack."

"Racine doesn't need a snack." Michael dropped the whole milk carton into Racine's tank. Then he swept the rest of the ants off his table and onto a sheet of notebook paper. He dropped the paper into the tank, too. "You made a mess. Stay away from Racine. I thought you didn't like him."

"He's sort of nice, with all those eyes. He threw hair at me."

"That's because he thought you were an enemy. You'd better start explaining what you were doing in here, anyway."

Celine almost said that a spider could always use an extra meal, when she smelled the sharp odor of lemons. "Do you smell lemon, Michael?"

"No."

"Lemon" starts with "L," like "liar," thought Celine. "Racine was right."

"What?"

"I was an enemy. I stole some roach wings and legs from him this morning."

Michael looked at Celine as if she were crazy. "Why?"

"I put them in my oatmeal."

Michael's face sagged. He looked slightly sick. "You didn't eat them, did you?"

"No." Celine laughed. "Of course not, dummy. I just showed my bowl to Ma, and she threw it all out. She didn't know I put the roach parts there."

"Why'd you do that?"

"So I could have something good for

breakfast. She let me make a bagel."

"Celine, what is the matter with you? Why don't you just tell Ma you hate oatmeal and you want to make your own breakfast from now on?"

"I can't do that."

"Give me one good reason why not."

Celine raised her shoulders, then dropped them in exasperation. "You're the big one, not me. She'd just think I was making trouble."

"And roach parts in oatmeal isn't trouble?" Michael put his hand on Celine's shoulder. "I hate to break it to you, sis, but you're totally nuts."

Angel Talk

"Have you been whispering in Michael's ear?" asked the archangel.

The Little Angel of Honesty shook her head. "He just came in on his own. I haven't seen him since this morning on the playground. But he sure does know the right thing to say."

The archangel nodded. "And what was all that about Ellen smelling lemons and Celine shouting she hated them and then Celine smelling lemons?"

The little angel gave a small smile. "I'm not sure, but I have a guess. I put lemon drops in front of Ellen's nose. And when Ellen talked about them, Celine got all worried. I think she associates the smell of lemons with being called a liar. So I put lemon drops in front of her nose when she was talking to Michael— hoping the smell would make her not want to be called a liar again, so she'd tell the truth, instead." The little angel puffed her chest out in triumph. "And she did tell the truth—so my lemon drops work."

"You can't walk around holding lemon drops in front of Celine's nose all the rest of her life, though."

The little angel put her hand in her pocket and came out with a small fistful of spider hairs. She spread them on her other palm. They looked fluffy, but really they felt prickly. She smiled at the archangel. "No, not the rest of her life. But maybe a few more times. Just until she gets used to saying what's really on her mind."

Revelations

"Celine? Michael? I'm home." Ma came into the kitchen and rested a big shopping bag on a chair. Then she looked around. "What are you doing? You can't eat that junk before dinner."

Michael spread peanut butter on a square of a Hershey's chocolate bar and put it in his mouth. Then he prepared another square and handed it to Celine.

"Stop it, Michael. It's bad enough you're spoiling your own appetite. Don't ruin your sister's."

Michael looked at Celine.

Celine held the chocolate square in her fingers and hesitated. Then she smelled that smell again. "Lemon!" she shouted. She ate the chocolate and peanut butter.

"Celine. Honestly, didn't you hear me?" Ma screwed the lid onto the peanut butter jar.

Celine took a deep breath of lemon. "I needed it, Ma. I needed this junk food. And you know what? This morning I put those roach parts in my oatmeal so I wouldn't have to eat it."

Ma's eyes opened wide. Her mouth froze in a little o. Then she slowly sat down. "I didn't know you hated oatmeal."

"I don't really hate it. Sometimes I love it. But I want to choose what I eat for breakfast."

"Oh. Well." Ma looked relieved. "As long as you choose a good, healthful meal, I guess that's okay."

"Really?" Celine unscrewed the lid of the peanut butter jar again.

"But eating junk before dinner is a different thing." Ma pulled the jar back toward her and put the lid on. "I'm glad you told me about breakfast."

"That's not all Celine wants to tell you

about," said Michael. He looked meaningfully at Celine.

Celine took another deep breath. Sure enough, her nostrils filled with the tartness of lemons. "I bought overalls."

Ma leaned forward and opened her mouth. Then she froze again. She closed her mouth and sat tall and prim. "Tell me more."

"I used my own money. From allowances. I saved up. And I wore them to school today."

"But I saw you leave for school in your nice black skirt with the red ladybugs."

"I changed on the way."

Ma cleared her throat. "I see."

"I love them. I can do rolls on the grass in them without even getting hurt. And the pockets are big enough to hold everything."

Ma nodded. "Well, where are they?"

"I hid them."

"Looks like this is a day of revelations." Ma slowly smiled. "So go on. Go get them and model these wonderful pants for me."

Angel Talk

"You've done a good job, little angel."
The Archangel of Honesty kissed the little angel on the forehead. "And much faster than I expected."

"I'm not finished. When Celine was talking with her mother, I put lemon drops in front of her nose. She kept breathing lemon."

The archangel pursed her lips. "I thought she was on her own."

"I saw her hesitate—and I knew she needed the lemon smell." The little angel shook her head. "No, I'm not done till she can tell the truth without any help from me."

"It's hard, isn't it?" said the archangel very softly.

"Telling the truth without any kind of deception at all? Yes," said the little angel. "It's hard. For anyone."

The archangel hugged the little angel. "You seem to understand Celine pretty well now."

"I think I do. Celine deceived her mother because she felt powerless. Learning that she has rights was hard for her." The little angel sighed. "Learning that you have a right to be whoever you are, whether you're boring or interesting, is hard, too."

"Are you talking about Celine, still? Or someone else?"

"I'm not sure," whispered the little angel.

The Last Whiff

The doorbell rang.

Celine ran for it. "Hi, Cara."

"I smell lemon." Cara wrinkled her nose. "I can't get it out of my nose. It led me here."

"My middle name's not Susie," said Celine.

"What?"

"Did the lemon smell go away?" asked Celine.

Cara sniffed. Then she smiled. "Yes. What do you know."

"Go home." Celine started to shut the door.

"Wait. If your middle name's not Susie, why do you want to be called Susie?"

"I don't. I mean, I did. Susie's a nice name. And it doesn't sound like a spider. But now I like the spider, so I'm happy to be called Celine."

Cara blinked. Then she slowly turned and walked away.

Celine shut the door.

The doorbell rang.

Celine opened the door. "Oh, Mrs. Marcy. Don't tell me you smell lemons."

"I don't," said Mrs. Marcy. "Should I?"

"No." Celine felt herself blush. "Sorry. I just thought . . . well, it doesn't matter."

"I came by to see if I could help you set up your new ant farm."

"Actually, Mrs. Marcy, I fed the ants to my brother's spider."

Mrs. Marcy's face lost all its color.

"I'm sorry. But he was hungry."

Mrs. Marcy didn't say anything.

"And it was my fault he was hungry. See? I should have told you on the playground, but I didn't want to upset you. I'm sorry you came all the way over here for nothing."

"Well, that's all right," said Mrs. Marcy at last. "Good-bye."

"Wait. Are you sure you didn't smell lemons?"

"Yes, I'm sure. Why? Do you smell lemons?"

Celine took a deep breath. "No." She laughed. "Isn't it wonderful?"

Angel Thoughts

The Little Angel of Honesty emptied one pocket of all the spider hairs. Then she emptied her other pocket. It had a family of glass spiders. She'd bought them in a store near the beach—a store that sold things from Venice, Italy—right there in Venice, California.

The little angel had planned to take the real spider hairs along with those glass spiders back to her friends and let them come to their own conclusions. Like always. They'd think she was really important, even though she was the littlest angel. Like always.

But now that plan didn't seem so good.

The little angel didn't want the other angels to think she was important for all the wrong reasons. She was who she was. And she liked

who she was. And maybe if the other angels knew who she really was, they might like her, anyway.

The little angel puffed out her cheeks and blew away the spider hairs. Then she picked up the glass spiders and dropped them in an empty metal garbage can. The fine legs broke with a high, tinkling noise, like a tiny bell.

Now the little angel filled her pockets instead with the small carved wooden balls she'd bought in a different store—a store that sold only goods made from California trees. These balls were some kind of evergreen, but they smelled like cinnamon. The other angels would love them.

A strange sensation warmed the angel. New feathers sprouted thick and white all over her wings. Flight was hers, at long last.

The newest Archangel of Honesty took to the skies, ready to deliver her gifts truthfully.

How to care for your pet spider

Hairy spiders like Racine are not cuddly pets, but they can be interesting to watch. If you want to keep one as a pet, here are some things you'll need:

• a glass tank, ten gallons or larger, depending on how big your spider is going to grow
• a screen to put on the top of the tank, so the spider doesn't crawl out
• a light mounted somewhere in the tank to provide heat for spider (You can turn the light off at night.)
• bark or Astroturf for the bottom of the tank (You should clean it once a week.)
• branches for the spider to climb on and hide in (these should be changed every other week)
• live insects to eat (If you don't want to catch insects yourself, pet stores will sell you crickets by the dozen. You can drop in a few, and the spider will eat them whenever he's hungry. Don't worry if your spider eats three crickets one day and nothing for the next few days. That's normal for a hairy spider.)

Meet the Little Angel of Responsibility
in the next *Angelwings*

№ 10 Running Away

I don't like that mother," said the little angel.

"What? Why not?"

"She made Danielle go shopping with her instead of letting Danielle do her homework."

"Now wait just a minute." The Archangel of Responsibility scratched the very top of his head. When he did that, he looked taller than ever. "You saw the same thing I saw. The mother wanted everyone to help her shop, sure, but she didn't force Danielle."

"But they could have gone shopping later, after Danielle finished her homework. Now Danielle's going to get in trouble with her teacher."

"You're right about the teacher part," said the archangel.

"I'm right about the mother, too," said the Little Angel of Responsibility firmly. "She's the irresponsible one."

"Come on. The mother asked Danielle if she had homework."

The Little Angel of Responsibility looked away in confusion. She'd been wondering herself about why Danielle hadn't told her mother she had homework to do. Still, the mother's behavior was what bothered her most. "What's so important about buying all those things, anyway? Bunches of grapes and plums. Is Danielle's mother crazy or something?"

"Sort of. That show she talked about worries her. She's going to put her photographs on exhibit, and she thinks of it as her big break—her chance to become a professional photographer."

"Oh." The little angel hesitated. "Oh, I get it now," she said with sympathy. "Does Danielle know that her mother's worried?"

"Yes."

So that's why Danielle didn't tell her

mother she had homework. "Well, then," said the little angel, "Danielle was right to go shopping with her mother." She nodded her head emphatically. "And there's really no job for me here. Danielle is being very responsible. Her mother needs her."

"She needs her, all right, little angel. But what she needs most right now is for Danielle to do all the things she's supposed to do. Danielle's mother is counting on her to have her schoolwork done."

"Now we're back to where we started. The mother shouldn't make Danielle go shopping when it's time to do homework."

"But she thinks Danielle already did her homework," said the archangel. "Danielle made her think that."

"Danielle didn't actually lie," said the Little Angel of Responsibility slowly.

"Does it matter? Danielle knows what her mother thinks. She does have a problem, little angel, and you do have a job here."

Read all of the
Aladdin *Angelwings* stories:

№. 1

Friends Everywhere
0-689-82694-X

№. 2

Little Creatures
0-689-82695-8

№. 3

On Her Own
0-689-82985-X

№ 4

One Leap Forward
0-689-82986-8

№ 5

Give and Take
0-689-83205-2

№ 6

No Fair!
0-689-83206-0

All titles $3.99 US / $5.50 Canadian

Aladdin Paperbacks
Simon & Schuster Children's Publishing
www.SimonSaysKids.com

And don't miss these other
Aladdin *Angelwings* stories:

№. 7

April Flowers
0-689-83207-9
$3.99 US
$5.50 Canadian

№. 8

Playing Games
0-689-83208-7
$3.99 US
$5.50 Canadian